# Fighting Dragons

# Fighting Dragons

## Colin West

**WALKER
BOOKS**

First published 1995 by Walker Books Ltd
87 Vauxhall Walk, London SE11 5HJ

This edition published 2017

2 4 6 8 10 9 7 5 3 1

This book has been typeset in Garamond

Printed in Great Britain by Clays Ltd, St Ives plc

British Library Cataloguing in Publication Data:
a catalogue record for this book is available from the British Library

ISBN 978-1-4063-7875-7

www.walker.co.uk

# CONTENTS

# CHAPTER ONE

Long, long ago, in a cottage in the woods, lived little Katy with her mum and dad.

Every morning at half past eight
Katy's dad, dressed in his suit of
armour and with his armour-plated
lunch box, left for work.

Every night at six o'clock, Katy's dad came home. Over tea he told Katy and her mum about his day.

11

He told of fighting fierce dragons,

and of winning jousting tournaments.

He told of rescuing princesses,

and of wrestling with wild wolves.

For Katy's dad had a job as a
knight at the nearby castle.

Ye Olde Nearby Castle

Katy loved hearing about her
dad's daring deeds. But she was
sometimes sad, for she longed for a
slice of the action.

Alack! Alas! Alackaday!

Everyone said that Katy was too young to fight dragons – and who'd ever heard of a little girl winning jousting tournaments? But little Katy was determined, and she worked out a crafty plan.

# CHAPTER TWO

One morning, Katy wrote a note for her mum, which she left on her dressing-table.

Then, when her dad left for work at half past eight, Katy crept out of the back door.

She followed her father from a
safe distance.

"When I catch up with him, it will
be too late to send me home,"
thought Katy. "He'll have to let me
stay with him."

That was Katy's plan, anyway.

Katy's dad went through the woods, over the bridge, across the turnip field, over the stile, and he turned left at the crossroads.

Katy was a little way behind.

"He's heading for the castle," she said to herself. "He must be going to get his orders from the king."

The castle came into view and
Katy's dad went over the drawbridge
and under the portcullis.

Katy ran a little faster. She mustn't lose sight of her dad inside the castle walls.

She passed over the drawbridge, but came to a halt when a guard asked where she was going.

I've come to help my dad fight dragons.

The guard chuckled to himself and let her pass.

Katy rushed into the side entrance after her father. She followed the sound of his footsteps along a narrow corridor and down a steep stone staircase.

At the bottom, she caught sight of him just before he disappeared behind a big door hung on huge hinges.

Katy reached the door, which creaked loudly as she pushed it open.

Her dad's face went white when he saw her.

"I've come to help you fight dragons," Katy announced.

"B… b… but fighting dragons is dangerous work," her dad said. "You must go home at once – and that's final!" he added firmly.

# CHAPTER THREE

Katy was sorry her plan hadn't worked, and she sniffed as she held back a tear.

It was then that she noticed something odd.

Her father had
come to a tiny
room which was
stacked high with
dirty pots and pans
and platters.

Just then a man
wearing an apron
came by with a big
pile of plates.

"Good morning, George," he said
to Katy's dad. "You've got a busy
time ahead of you today."

Katy's dad blushed bright pink.

"Has he got an extra big dragon
to fight?" asked Katy.

The man in the apron laughed so
much he almost dropped the plates.

"No, silly!" he chortled. "The king
had a banquet last night. There's an
extra lot of washing-up today!"

Katy's dad blushed an even brighter red.

The man in the apron put down the pile of plates and went away, still laughing.

Katy's dad sat down, took off his helmet and put Katy on his knee.

"I've got a confession to make," he said, clearing his throat.

I'm not really a knight who fights dragons – I'm just a washer-upper at the castle!

Katy was flabbergasted. Her brave daddy a humble washer-upper? She couldn't believe it.

But her dad explained things...

A long time ago, before you were born, your mum fancied a flashy knight named Kevin.

The only way I could win her over was to pretend to be even more dashing.

So I made up stories about fighting dragons and saving princesses from evil enemies.

It all got out of hand, and I couldn't admit the truth — that I'm a washer-upper at the castle.

And so I've been dressing up in armour pretending to be a knight for her ever since.

"It's quite a task wearing armour all the while, you know," he said.

Katy had a lump in her throat. She could see her dad looked really ashamed.

"I bet you're a good washer-upper, though," she said cheerfully.

The best—
even if I say
so myself!

Her dad puffed up with pride. "I get every cup and saucer spotless."

"Don't worry, then," said Katy.

I'll keep your secret, but I would ask one thing...

"What's that?" asked her dad.

Katy looked him in the eye.

"That you let me help out today, after all."

Her dad smiled broadly. "Done!" he said, shaking her hand.

# CHAPTER FOUR

Katy and her dad got to work on the
piles of washing-up.

Katy's dad soaped them
thoroughly and Katy dried them up.

They made a good team and only
stopped once – to share the
sandwiches from the armour-plated
lunch box. By twenty past five
they'd got through all the piles of
washing-up. Every pot and pan and
knife and fork was sparkling clean.

"Thanks for helping!" said Katy's dad as he dried his hands. "We can go home ten minutes early now."

The two of them walked up the stone steps, along the narrow corridor, through the side entrance, under the portcullis and over the drawbridge.

They turned right at the crossroads
and went over the turnip field.

But halfway across, they suddenly came face to face with a fearsome sight.

Before them stood the biggest,
fiercest, meanest-looking
dragon ever. He was
breathing fire and
burping smoke.
Katy and her dad
quaked in their boots.

Katy did the first thing that came to mind. She chucked her dad's armour-plated lunch box at the monster's ugly head.

She was a good shot and the lunch box hit the dragon right between the eyes.

He staggered around in a daze.

Then Katy stamped on the
dragon's feet.

It made him hopping mad.

Katy's dad pulled the dragon's tail. It made him wail with pain.

Then Katy kicked the dragon's bottom.

This was the last straw for the dragon, who went bounding off back to his cave.

"That was a close shave," sighed Katy's dad, mopping his brow.

"That was *fun*!" said Katy with a grin.

# CHAPTER FIVE

Katy and her father dusted
themselves down and continued
their homeward journey.

They merrily walked down the lane and through the woods and arrived home at six o'clock on the dot.

"Hello, Katy. I'm glad you're safe, but you must never go off like that again."

I'm sorry, Mum, but we had an important job to do. We fought the BIGGEST, FIERCEST, MEANEST-LOOKING DRAGON ever!

"Is that so?" smiled Katy's mum. "You must tell me about it over tea."

So over scrambled eggs and beans
Katy and her dad told how they...

chucked the armour-plated
lunch box at the dragon's head,

and how they stamped on the
dragon's feet,

and how they pulled the dragon's tail,

and how they kicked the dragon's bottom, until they sent him bounding off back to his cave.

"Well done, both of you!" said Katy's mum. "Now who'll do the washing-up?"

Katy's dad winked at Katy and they got to work on the dishes again.

They got through the washing-up
quickly and Katy was soon tucked
up in bed after her amazing day.

Her dad kissed her good night
and whispered in her ear, "Thanks
for keeping my secret."

Then Katy's mum came in to kiss her good night, too.

"That was a fine story you made up about the dragon," she said.

But it was true, Mum!

Her mum smiled. "I know the truth," she sighed.

I know your father washes up at the castle and that he's never fought dragons in his life!

"But, Mum, we really did fight a fearsome dragon today!" insisted Katy.

Her mother smiled.

"If you say so, dear," she said. "Good night, Katy."

"Good night, Mum," said Katy.

Katy nodded off to sleep, ready
to dream of fighting fierce dragons,
or getting through piles of washing-
up. Who's to know?

**Colin West** has written and illustrated lots of books for young readers. These include a series of stories about a hippo called Howard and another about a dog called Monty, which has been turned into an animated television series. Among his many popular picture book titles are *"Have you seen the crocodile?"* and four other jungle tales plus four animal stories: *"Only Joking!" Laughed the Lobster, One Day in the Jungle, "I Don't Care!" Said the Bear* and *"Buzz, Buzz, Buzz," went Bumblebee.* Colin is also the author of several collections of poetry, and his verses have been broadcast on radio and television.